FOXY

and Friends go Racing

First published in hardback in Great Britain by HarperCollins Publishers Ltd in 1998

First published in Picture Lions in 1998
1 3 5 7 9 10 8 6 4 2
ISBN 0 00 664565-8

Picture Lions is an imprint of the Children's Division, part of HarperCollins Publishers Ltd.
Text and illustrations copyright © Colin and Jacqui Hawkins 1998
The author/illustrators assert the moral right to be identified as the
author/illustrators of the work.

Printed and bound in Singapore by Imago.

FOXY
and Friends go Racing

Colin and Jacqui Hawkins

PictureLions
An Imprint of HarperCollinsPublishers

Foxy and his friends, Dog and Badger,
were watching television.
"I'm going to be a racing car driver
when I grow up," said Foxy.
"So am I," said Badger.
"And me," said Dog.
"Copycats," said Foxy's little sister.
"I'm going to be a doctor."
"No one asked you,"
said Foxy.

Later that morning, Foxy and his friends
were busy in the garden shed.
Foxy's little sister was very curious.
"What are you doing?" she asked.
"Can I play?"
"No you can't," said Foxy.
"Go away!"
So off she went to
play doctors with
Teddy.

Inside the shed the friends
worked very hard.
Foxy sawed...

RASP!
RASP!

Dog hammered...
BANG!
BANG!

Badger painted...

DRIP!
DRIP!

Until they had built their very own supersonic racing car.

"We'll need helmets," said Foxy.
"All racing car drivers wear them."
They found some helmets in the kitchen.

"And goggles," said Dog, putting on his swimming goggles.

"And gloves," said Badger, pulling on a pair of rubber gloves.

The friends set off for the park to try out
their new racing car.
"Phew!" puffed Dog, as they
pushed it up the great
big hill.

At the top they all scrambled into the car.

READY,
STEADY,
GO!

The car quickly gathered speed.
"This is great!" shouted Foxy.

WHEE!

They zoomed down the hill.
"Brake!" cried Foxy.
"Where?" yelled Badger.
"Oh! Noooo!" howled Dog.
The car hurtled on, faster and
faster, until…

THWACK!

The racing car struck a large stone…

and threw the friends high up into the air.

HELP!

Foxy, Badger and Dog crashed to the ground.

"OOOOH! My head," whined Dog.

"OOOOH! My poor paw," groaned Badger.

"OOOOH! I hurt all over," moaned Foxy.

"Do you need a doctor?"
someone said.
It was Foxy's little sister
with her doctor's bag.
"Don't worry, this
won't hurt," she said.
She put sticky plasters on cuts and grazes.

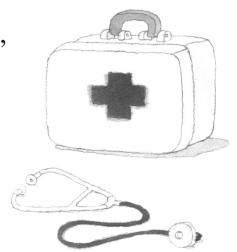

She rubbed ointment on bumps and lumps, and wrapped bandages around scratches and scrapes.

Soon everyone felt much better. "Thanks Doc!" they all said.

"What shall we do now?" said Badger. "I know," said Foxy, "let's all play doctors."

And for the rest of the day, they had lots of fun racing the ambulance up and down the great big hill.

But first, they made sure their new
ambulance had a brake!
"I'm going to be an ambulance
driver when I grow up," said Foxy.
"So am I," said Badger.
"And me," said Dog.
"Copycats!" giggled
Foxy's little sister.

Collect all the stories about
FOXY

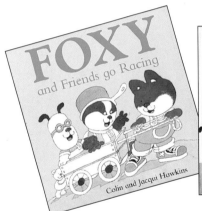

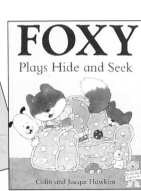

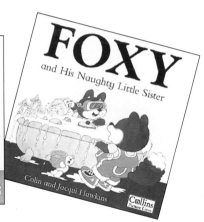